W9-CHR-540

STEVE
THE ALIEN

By G. Brian Benson

Illustrated by Paul Hernandez

STEVE THE ALIEN
By G. Brian Benson

Cover design and illustrations by Paul Hernandez

FIRST EDITION

"Happily expect the unexpected."

– G. Brian Benson

Here lies a tale you might find hard to be true

But true it is, and true it was, so let's give it its due!

I don't want any doubters. Does everyone believe?

It's the truest of the true. There are no tricks up my sleeve!

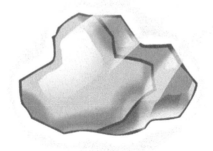

This story took place not quite one year ago

As I was walking to school in three feet of snow.

I was huffing and puffing as I struggled to walk

When I looked to the sky and saw what looked like a big rock.

It was shiny and shimmering against the sun's brightest rays

As it dodged a few clouds on that cold wintry day.

It made a soft buzz, like a large swarm of bees.

I had nowhere to go! I wanted to flee!

My wits became frazzled as I realized what was near!

A small UFO approached (which instilled such big fear!)

It landed quite gently in a snow drift nearby.

What was this strange thing that came down from the sky?

I stared quite intently, wondering what might be next

But nothing was happening. I was scared and quite vexed!

Would a monster come out with four legs and eight arms?

With horns and sharp teeth, intent to do me some harm?

13

I braced for the worst as a door opened wide.

I dearly was wishing I had somewhere to hide!

But since that couldn't happen, I tried to act tough.

So I stood on my tiptoes and snarled to look gruff.

My eyes got big and I gasped for some air

As I watched a green being climb down from the stairs.

He was short and was stout, about four feet tall

With three eyes, two arms, and two feet that were small.

He had one pair of antennae that flopped to and fro

Back and forth on his head in a true rhythmic flow.

His body was covered in clothes that stood out

All silver and shiny, quite flashy no doubt.

He then walked toward me in a shuffling way

I thought about running, but decided to stay.

This curious thing seemed friendly to me.

Not quite sure why, but I would wait here and see.

He then stopped before me and raised his right arm

And said, "My name is Steve and I mean you no harm."

I couldn't believe that this alien spoke!

If this was a dream, I still hadn't woke!

"Hello Steve," said I, "my name is Zeke.

Welcome to Earth, and how did you learn to speak?"

"I learned in a school just like you do.

I speak French, German, and Japanese too!"

"But the reason I'm here and I have no time to lose

I have come to your planet to try to find shoes."

"Try to find shoes?" I said, taken aback.

"You've come to the right place, for shoes we don't lack!"

"Why do you need shoes? What's going on?"

I said in a voice both forceful and strong.

He replied with a smirk and a tilt of his head,

"I've entered a contest with my good friend Ned."

"It's a scavenger hunt across the great sky

And to win first place we're encouraged to try!"

"How cool is that!" said Zeke, with a smile.

"How far have you traveled? How many miles?"

"I've been to twenty-one planets and five different stars

When I leave here from Earth, my next stop is Mars.

But to answer in miles, I haven't a clue,

I finally stopped counting at five billion and two."

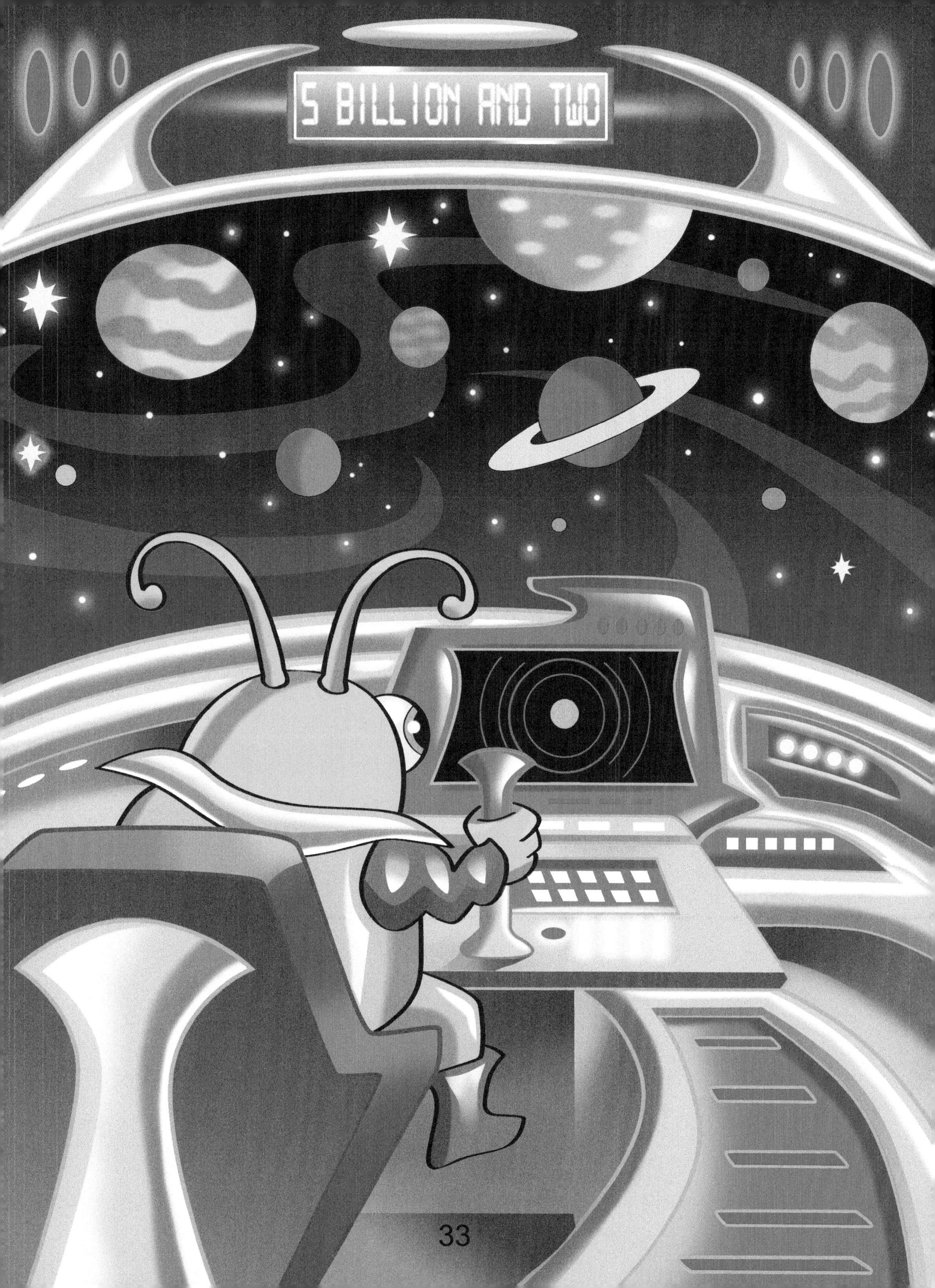
5 BILLION AND TWO

"How long have you been gone from your planet?" I squeaked.

"Just eight and a half hours," said Steve, rather meek.

"My ship is quite old and lacks turbo blast

And I just got my license and not allowed to go fast."

My head was spinning as Steve told his story

Of traveling through space to win intergalactic glory.

This was just like a dream, had I not been awake.

I wish I'd had my camera to prove this wasn't fake!

"So do you have some shoes I could take back with me?"

Said Steve rather rushed, "For my scavenger spree?"

"Most definitely, for sure" as I set down my pack.

"They are orange with spikes and I use them for track."

"Why thank you," said Steve, as I handed them over

To his green little fingers, the color of clover.

He turned around and walked back to his ship

All shiny and bright, ultra cool and extra hip.

"Good luck!" I yelled, as he climbed up the stairs.

He turned, waved, and smiled with an alien flair.

Steve shut the door to his supersonic craft

And fired up the engines which created a draft.

I took a step back as he launched into space

My head again spinning from what just took place.

Will anyone believe me? Will anyone care

About my close encounter, so crazy and rare?

45

I could see a faint glimpse of his ship way up high

And thought to myself, what would it be like to fly?

Will he be back again, some other cold day?

Or stay up in the heavens to fly and to play?

47

Maybe one day you'll be walking to school

And hear a soft buzz, from a spacecraft so cool.

Please make sure and say "Hi!" to my green friend, Steve

And give him your shoes, which he comes to retrieve.

CPSIA information can be obtained
at www.ICGtesting.com
Printed in the USA
FSOW04n0710171016
26109FS

9 780982 228685